COURTING DEATH

COURTING DEATH

LIVIA HARDY

authorHOUSE®

AuthorHouse™ UK Ltd.
1663 Liberty Drive
Bloomington, IN 47403 USA
www.authorhouse.co.uk
Phone: 0800.197.4150

Published by AuthorHouse 09/01/2014

ISBN: 978-1-4969-8656-6 (sc)
ISBN: 978-1-4969-8867-6 (e)

Cover illustration by Clonefront Entertainment
Illustrator: Rachel Lester
Art director: Arpad Olbey
http://clonefront.co.uk
info@clonefront.co.uk

This book is printed on acid-free paper.

1

"JOHNNY'S ALWAYS RUNNING around ..." sang Alex as he ran along. In and out of traffic, through the racing lines of cars. His body was controlling him: leap this way, spring that way, terrify the drivers. Alex was lucky the busy A road was so close to his home. He lived on the outskirts of town, and it was literally just the other side of the motorway. A couple of years ago, it had all been very different. It had been a small road with slow-moving queues full of people waiting for their turn at the lights, all striving to get to work on time. Alex had spent some of his mornings there even then, just watching the cars. He had never been able to explain the fascination he had felt at that time. There had been no adrenaline rush, no passion, just an unquenchable thirst to gaze at the vehicles unendingly. Now he spent all his mornings there, or most of them anyway, and he wondered whether it was the years of taking in cars, their movement, their speed, and drivers' reactions that made him so good at this sport.

Death looked on silently and smiled. Yes, yes. Alex was always running around! He grinned as he watched Alex nearly kill himself and then escape just in time. Yes, Alex was getting very good at this, and he would have to be rewarded in some way. He watched for a few more minutes, casting a dark cloud and a chill over the road; then he turned his attention to planning the reward and poking his nose into Mischief's business.

Alex was running out in front of a big lorry that was rapidly gaining on him. As it was just about to hit him, he rolled out of the way, into the dirty gutter, panting as the sound of a horn rang in his ears. He lay there exhausted for a few minutes, just absorbing the details of the cars speeding past him. Then, picking up his spirits, he jumped out to the next line of cars, in front of a beautiful motorbike, a Honda Goldwing. The tyres screeched; the driver nearly fell off his bike. He swore violently at Alex, who laughed and quickly jumped onto the back of a passing Jeep. He jumped off again when they had lost the motorbike and stopped at a traffic light. Had it not been rush hour, Alex could have spent the day trying to escape a furious driver. Rush hour provided the certainty Alex needed that nobody had time to try and catch the fifteen-year-old.

Alex was in a completely different part of town now. He was quite near where Lilly-Rose Mac Henners lived. Silly brat! She was probably in school now, giggling about something stupid with her friends. He wasn't one to go to school every day and get told off by the teacher. He had left his house early that morning with his packed lunch, and he had no idea how or when he was going to get back home. He did not care about that either. His friend Neil would assure his mother that he was at Neil's house having fun and that he'd come back as soon as they had finished. His mother generally left it at that, and when she did not, he'd bring out a few leftover pieces of one of Neil's model aeroplanes, which they had supposedly been making, and then she'd believe him.

He always had a nagging feeling deep, deep down, something that could only be described as resentment, when he thought about his mother. Alex wasn't quite sure what it was he resented about her or her attitude. Or was it her lack of attitude? Something about the way she accepted his excuses stirred up a fierce anger inside of him. Surely she knew he wasn't at school or at Neil's house or, in fact, anywhere else he said he was. She must know something was wrong, that he wasn't her little boy anymore. And yet, a simple piece of plastic made her stop questioning him and leave him in peace. She'd been like that for a while now. He knew when it had started. He had blocked her out … he and Jay … but the painful memories that arose when he remembered Jay were what made him carry on ignoring his mother, living only in the present.

He strolled along the pavement admiring the beautiful trees that bedecked it. Lilly-Rose certainly did not live in a run-down part of town. Soon he was in sight of her house. Should he play a trick on her mother or not? No, her mother probably worked, so it would just be a waste of time. He turned away from the house and looked at the road. Taunting death amongst the cars was getting to be boring, so he considered what else he could do. He looked up at the edge of the flyover that went over the motorway, and he smiled. He was an ace in gymnastics – at least he used to be. Was he still, though? Well, he'd soon see!

Alex walked to the edge of the flyover and climbed up onto the side. As soon as he was up, he felt himself wobble violently, and there was a lot of angry beeping from the passing cars. He quickly regained his balance and started off along the edge slowly. Soon he was three metres off the ground and endeavouring not to look down or misplace his foot and fall off. He finally found his balance and sighed with great satisfaction. He had started going more quickly now, but he stopped opposite Lilly-Rose's house and tried to see inside. He almost fell down in surprise! There she was, on the telephone and pointing at him! He looked down on one side and saw that he was about four metres up now, over a busy road. On the other side the cars were driving past very quickly, but there was a little pavement only a metre or so lower than him. He jumped down and crouched so that he could only just see Lilly-Rose. She was still on the phone and she was gesturing wildly with her arms as though she were using them to keep her balance, which was what he had been doing! He ran along bent double and reached the other end of the flyover. Alex suddenly smiled to himself and thought that if she was going to be a brat, he would be one too. He knew exactly what would make her afraid. He'd have to go home first and phone from his landline. She knew his mobile number off by heart.

On his way home, he thought through his little plan. It was just a silly game, but it might worry her. He would make her think she was in the middle of something. A plot, an important plot. He would phone her and pretend to be a gang member and pass on a number to her. If she dialled it repeatedly and bothered someone enough, they might report her and send the police over! She was still on the phone when he got home, so he waited a while, lying on his bed and leafing through the telephone book. He stopped at a number he found interesting and circled it with the pen; then he tried her house again.

"Mademoiselle Lillie?" Yes, it was her; she sounded confused. Perhaps she did not know any French people. Alex had to go on. He gave her the number he had picked out of the directory and told her to phone there asking for messages for "Petit Pierre" and, the third time, to ask for Marie-Louise. She collected her wits fast enough to ask why, and he told her that they'd give her the next set of instructions. They did not, of course, but they did use enough swear words to make her feel threatened. That would take up some of her precious time, he thought. It was a classic schoolboy prank, yet Alex was sure she was too curious not to fall for it. He sighed as he closed the front door and started off down the road again, feeling slightly uneasy until he had a new thought: to finish off the day he could go to the river.

Death sat there watching Alex's every move in fascinated silence. He was inching his way across the very narrow drainpipe that crossed the river at its most dangerous point. Death chuckled. He merely had to click his fingers, and Alex would immediately fall in and kill himself. His clenched hand opened. His middle finger and his thumb got ready to click. His heart was beating faster and faster. It stopped. He realised that he could not kill Alex. What would be the point of that?

As Alex approached the middle, he felt as if someone were watching him. He shuddered. He'd had that feeling before – as though someone were walking on his grave – but he hadn't ever felt it as strongly as this. He tried to remember exactly when he'd felt it. He could not remember exactly, yet he was sure that he had felt it a couple of times. But what was it? He shook his head and continued to cross. It was a rather wide river, and he was going onto the island around which it flowed. In summer the island was beautiful, covered in wild flowers, and many people would visit, but – as there was no bridge – they had to use boats. The island was inaccessible in winter. There was only the drainpipe attaching it to the mainland, but, as it was around the back, overgrown side of the island, no one had ever noticed it except for him. And nobody would have dared use it to cross even if they had seen it.

Alex was nearly at the shore when the terrible feeling came back, much stronger than before, but he firmly pushed it to the back of his mind until he had put his feet on solid ground. Once he was on the island, the feeling disappeared. This was his place of peace, a bittersweet stillness. He wandered around slowly until he found the place where he used to come with Jay. She had been his best friend for what had seemed like forever – but then she died. He had been with her. He had seen her die. He had been unable to help her. He had sat and held her for a few minutes, which had seemed like an eternity, but as the sirens had approached, he'd made himself scarce. Fear had taken over, and he panicked, knowing that he would be blamed. He already felt ashamed, and alone, and lost.

Sure enough, Jay's parents had wasted no time in accusing him. They had gone so far as to claim it was murder, premeditated murder. That had hurt. The guilt and sadness he felt had overwhelmed him from the moment she died; then the accusations had started coming from every direction. Even his mum had looked at him with anger and blamed him. He knew it was his fault. Jay had been out running in the traffic with him, and a car had hit her. It had not hit him.

That was it! It was at that moment he had felt the same strange feeling of being watched, just as she had screamed and fallen. He remembered now very clearly; the images came back, the emotions overwhelmed him once again, and it was too much for him. He fled from the memories.

When he arrived back at the pipe, his head had cleared; he shouldn't think about it while he crossed, but he did. Jay had been his everything, his life. They had got on perfectly from day one. He smiled to himself as he climbed up the steep bend in the pipe. He could remember her smile on the first day she walked into class. It was cheeky, daring, full of life and joy. He'd known then that they would get on. And they had! After a couple of weeks of class – he hadn't missed a day that week – they'd already moved round the classroom in order to sit next to each other. By the first half term, they'd been best friends.

Alex continued over the pipe, reliving the first time he'd shown her what he really spent his time doing. His friends had all laughed at him and at their friendship, all the "Alex and Jay, sitting in a tree ..." renditions came out. Alex shrugged them away; he hadn't cared and neither had she. This was friendship and nothing more. Lilly-Rose had been at the centre of all the teasing. She had been wildly jealous of Jay and had tried to separate them any way she could. One day her taunting had irritated them enough that Jay had suggested they skip class.

"Give them something to talk about," she had said. Once out of school, she hadn't known where to go, so Alex had led her down to his favourite spot. It had become their meeting place and then her favourite spot too. And, ironically, that was where ... where she had been taken.

Alex's thoughts were suddenly charged with a deep sadness again, but this time he let the despair wash over him. It might work today. Of course it might not; it was the third time he had tried, and the times before, he had failed. He braced himself and tried to run across the drainpipe. As his feet touched the pipe at speed, they slipped. His arms flailed around desperately, looking for an object to grip. It was one of those reflexes that he hated and sorely regretted afterward, for it was the only thing that stopped him from falling into the water. As he stuck out his arms, his outstretched hand grabbed onto a branch, and he remained there, hanging over the water. He sighed. It was over. He'd never have the courage to let himself drop, and he knew it. He pulled himself up onto the branch and gazed down into the flowing river. Would he ever go to be with Jay? He slid down the trunk, sat down, and buried his head in his knees. He had tried so many times to kill himself and was weary of never succeeding. Jay had not tried, and she had managed beautifully. He had felt lonely ever since she'd left.

Alex stood up and stretched. He had fallen asleep under the tree and it was already getting dark. He ran to the motorway, and when he got to the other side, he tried his luck hitchhiking. When no one stopped, however, he leapt into the trailer of a slow car and travelled nearly all the way home in its comfort. He jumped out of it a few lights away from his house and went to Neil's. Neil let him in and gave him a very brief update on what had happened at school in exchange for details about Alex's day. Then Alex left, asking Neil to tell his mother, if she phoned, that he was on his way home.

Normally he arrived at Neil's house earlier than he did today and had time to chat. He had been friends with Neil since they were in year one, and, although they had never considered themselves best friends, they had always ended up in the same class and always had enough to talk about. Neil had been there for him when he had needed moral support. He grimaced as he remembered those many evenings spent together. There had been no small talk; in fact there had been no talk at all. They had just sat in silence, and Alex had allowed himself to cry. Neil had said nothing, but he had been there. His parents had popped in the first few evenings and tried to chat but had soon realised that the boys only needed dinner on a tray, which they had provided. Neil had provided the silent comfort and company Alex needed.

He was nearly home when he saw all the lights being turned on downstairs in his house and the door opening briskly. It was his mother, throwing out her lover. She did not realise that Alex knew about Jim, so he had to leave before Alex came home. He hid in the shadows as Jim teetered past. He was obviously drunk and was muttering things about "that son of yours". As soon as he was out of earshot, Alex slipped out of his dark corner and walked slowly up to his house. His mother was in the kitchen, singing softly and making his tea. She had stopped asking him a long while ago about school, so when he came in she continued singing. As he sat down to eat, she sat next to him.

"Lilly-Rose called earlier."

"Uhm," he replied, his mouth full of sausage.

"She wanted to make sure you were okay. She said you weren't at school today."

Alex remained silent.

"Alex?"

He put on an unconcerned face and continued eating. He had grown used to inventing credible lies quite fast, and he figured that if she could lie to Dad, then he could lie to her. This time, though, it was a tiny bit harder because Lilly-Rose might have proof that he had been out. He told his mum that he had been sick and had tried to hitchhike to get home, but the person who took him had turned around and gone the wrong way so he had ended up near Lilly-Rose's house. This was the moment he always felt uneasy. Surely she knew he was lying. She must have known it wouldn't take him this long to come home: he could have walked in half the time. Why did she say nothing? He waited, hurriedly eating his dessert as his mother shrugged and started cleaning the kitchen.

She either believed him or put on a very good show of doing so, and so he went up to his room to "do homework". He was really planning what he would do the next day and the day after. He was short on inspiration, so for the moment he was just jotting down ideas that came to him while he read one of his favourite books. It was a wonderful story, and if he read it immediately before going to bed, it gave him weird and fascinating dreams. Today though, he did not want dreams: he wanted projects for his next day of truancy. He was gripped and amazed by what Stan, the main character, did to keep busy.

By the time his dad came upstairs, Alex had managed to plan a full schedule for the next day and a half. He hid the paper under his pillow and took out a school book. Dad's head peered round the door and asked how he was. He was feeling better now, Alex said, and his dad left.

They did not have much of a relationship. Alex felt that his dad had never really wanted one. Then all of a sudden his dad had changed and had started asking him questions, looking at him searchingly. That was soon after Alex had met Jay. Alex had been too busy for him then. He had felt odd when his dad spoke to him, like he still thought Alex was a little boy. Probably his dad felt odd too; it had been fifteen years of silence between them, hardly more than grunts and nods. He didn't feel fifteen when he was out enjoying himself. He felt so much older, more mature, more dangerous! He could easily have been thirty, he thought, like all those guys in the films he watched. He sighed. His dad did not understand him and had now given up trying.

Alex suddenly thought of a wonderful idea: he could spend a few hours making a potion that he would put into his lunch drink, and he would share it with Lilly-Rose! If she died, he would make some more for himself, and if not, then she would just have been a guinea pig. He liked that idea a lot (she did look like a guinea pig), so he made haste to write it down before he could forget it. Alex hadn't quite figured out why he wanted her to die so much but then he hadn't put much thought into it either. She annoyed him, so she was the perfect person to play around with.

He could also perhaps run away for a weekend. Nowhere far – perhaps the island if he could get across there lugging a backpack. If not, he would camp on one side and go across during the day. He shivered and pulled his hoodie up.

Death now stood next to Alex, at his desk. He was guiding his thoughts as to the ingredients to put in the potion: nettles, pineapple juice to make it taste all right … He grinned to himself as he foresaw the effect it would have on poor Lilly-Rose. After completing the list of ingredients, he decided to call a meeting and invite a few friends over to help him plan out their part in Alex's next day and night.

Alex stretched out in his bed and turned over. His dreams were confusing; they would change and then circle back to the first one and then change again, and he could not make head nor tail of them. When he woke up, he was sweating, and he knew that he had dreamt about Jay. It was not unusual that he dreamt about her, but recently he had stopped doing it as often. He got up, stripped his sheet off the bed, and threw it on the floor. He turned his quilt over; his mum would sort it out the next day. Then he remembered all the things that he had dreamt about. Some of them were good ideas, but there were some that he would never dare do, like jump off the highest building in town. He thought that he could probably manage to get up there, but as to jumping off it … He shuddered and snuggled down into his quilt.

The eerie feeling of being watched came back, and he scanned the room before moving towards the window. It was still dark outside, and the wind was blowing softly. The window was open, and he stepped out onto the balcony. The ivy had grown very long, and it swirled around him in a dreamlike way. He went to the very edge of the balcony and looked over the railings, which appeared hazy and ethereal. He was so high off the ground. Would he die if he jumped? He did not even know if he wanted to die anymore.

Someone was in the room behind him. Alex swung slowly round and saw Jay. She had on her favourite baggy purple trousers and her usual tight-fitting white top. Her short black hair was as clean as ever, and her make-up was perfect, as usual. She was smiling at him. He asked her to out on a date, and she refused, still smiling. He looked at her and slowly climbed over the railing.

Death was still there. All of his attention was now focused on Alex's mind. As Alex's first leg went over the railing, Death started to smile. The smile grew and grew until Alex's body was falling down to the ground. At that point the grin disappeared, but the eyes gleamed with long-awaited excitement. His hands were tightly clenched; the blood-red fingernails dug into the palms of his hands, and he grimaced. His fingers suddenly moved, but he didn't click. Instead he let out an exasperated sigh. He couldn't do it! Not now, not yet.

Dreams, dreams, this was another one of them. Jumping from his balcony was a possibility, but it did not appeal to his sense of adventure so Alex did not add it to his list. It had been a very convincing dream, though, especially as he had woken up standing on the balcony with a stem of ivy in his hands. As he looked out over his back garden, he felt a shiver run down his back. The landscape was ghostly and misty although it was already eight o'clock in the morning. Alex closed the window and wished he could go back to sleep. His mother came running in, telling him to hurry up or he'd be late for school. He slowly got ready though he was still half in a daze. If he made that potion today, then he could go to school the next day. He'd have to forge a note saying that he had been ill, but, after all, two days away was very easily covered up by a bad cold or a virus. He set off right after breakfast with his father, but he left his dad at the bus stop and veered off to the left, towards school.

Once he was out of his dad's sight, his brisk walk slowed down to a thoughtful amble. It was shopping time! Lilies were tricky, but he knew where to get roses. The park on the way to school had lots of rose bushes. He was sure he could find a couple of petals there. After he had picked enough petals and had thrown in a rose leaf for good measure, Alex started back off up the road towards his house. It was risky, as his mother might see him, but that was the way to the woods. While walking, he remembered the flower shop on the corner of his road – would it be worth it to buy a lily? He had only chosen them as an ingredient because they were her name and their smell might attract her more to the drink. He entered the shop and asked about lilies. They were far too expensive for him, he decided. She wasn't worth it. He smiled at the shop assistant, said he'd be back later with his mother, and left hurriedly.

Now to sneak past his house unobserved, he thought. As it happened, his mother was just coming out of the drive, but she did not notice him crouching behind the parked cars as she manoeuvred her way into the constant flow of traffic going down their road. As he walked towards the woods, he ticked the flowers off his list. Now to get the mud – there was plenty of that in the woods, and there was sand there too. He wasn't sure whether he'd add this or not; it might make the drink a bit too gritty. His main problem, however, would be to find all the different kinds of weeds he'd chosen. He wandered through the wood, up near to the playground and the football pitch, back down again, and round the horses' paddock. When, after a few hours, he still could not find some of the plants, he decided to go without. He had brought some juice with him and a flask. He mixed them all up and tore the leaves roughly. Then he thought he'd add some grass to make it a bit greener.

Death sat on Alex's bed, carefully putting some more red varnish on his nails. From time to time he looked up at the clock hanging on Alex's wall. It was not often that Death had to wait; normally he was the one who was late, but he could on no account miss this appointment. He had been busy, but Death often was! He had stopped by a few places that morning and had even joined Alex in the woods. The plants Alex had picked were not exactly what he had planned, and a few extra ones had made their way into the drink. The door opened, and the long-awaited person came in, followed by Alex. Death almost leapt for joy. He greeted his friend in the warmest way he could and motioned towards the bed. He had called his friend in to observe – and to advise.

Alex crept inside and paused to listen at his mother's door. She was back, and, as he had expected, she wasn't alone. She wouldn't miss the food processor. He took it up to his room with the carton of pineapple juice. He opened the door and shivered. He had not left the window open and the radiator was on at its highest, yet it was cold in his bedroom. He glanced around his room briefly; the bedding he had been given a few years ago was still his favourite – dark blue with his favourite team's logo on it. He had once had posters up of all the players he liked, but those had made way for perfectly white walls, repainted the summer he turned fourteen. He smirked at that thought; it was the summer his dad had decided it was his last chance to be a proper father. He had come home with the paint and two brushes one lovely summer day and announced that they would be painting

Alex's room as a father-and-son team the next day. Alex had phoned Jay that evening to say their plans would have to be postponed. She had thought it was great that his dad wanted to spend time with him; Alex had never told her how boring it had been. He sighed.

Alex closed the door and set to work. He wanted to finish this soon, and then he'd lie low or go out again. He poured the contents of his flask into the jug and stepped outside to get some ivy to add to it. Then he turned the processor on. The appliance was old and made plenty of noise, and Alex was afraid that his mother would hear it – but she did not. When he had finished, he added extra juice to make it more liquid. It smelled all right, and if she did not like it, he wasn't against drinking a bit to show her that it was good. He could not stop himself laughing as he pictured her face when she tasted it. He wondered whether it was tasty and whether it stung like nettles. He hoped that it did. Alex passed it through a sieve as a last precaution. He didn't want Lilly-Rose to gag on a leaf before having drunk any!

Suddenly he heard his mother's voice. She was getting nearer. He pushed everything under the bed and hid in the wardrobe. He was a bit surprised when his door handle turned and his mother came in because he had expected her to be headed downstairs. Jim was behind her, and he surveyed the room. He shivered and told her to turn the heat up. She tried to but could not; neither could Jim. They left and shut the door behind them. Alex heard his mum muttering about being certain she'd heard noises from somewhere in the house. Jim suggested they go out for lunch, and soon afterwards Alex heard the front door slam. Alex was quite happy with this arrangement; he did not have to lie low anymore. As soon as he heard the key turn in the lock, he stepped out of his wardrobe and took the juice out from under his bed. Nothing had spilt. He carefully poured it into his flask, which he then put away in his lunch box.

The rest of the day went fast as he planned more things to do. He had expected it to drag, like many days did leading up to an event, but there was something in the air that kept his adrenaline pumping. He had sat back on his bed once the drink was safely tucked away out of sight, and his eyes had wandered again round his white walls. Not your ordinary teenager's walls, he thought. But he had nothing to replace the posters with; these walls were probably the only blank space he had. His brain certainly had none – it was so full of … well, stuff! He could see shadows on the walls where the sun shone through the window and the ivy swayed in the wind. One of the shadows looked like Jay. His heart leapt and his thoughts flew back again to the day of her funeral.

She had a beautiful ornate coffin: dark wood with gold handles and flowers engraved all the way around. It wasn't her style – it wasn't like her at all, Alex thought. Jay was simple and elegant, not ornate and complicated. She was Jay – there was no other way to describe her. His parents had refused to go to her funeral. Knowing that Jay's family blamed Alex, they chose to send a card and not risk angering the family more. But Alex couldn't stay away. He hadn't seen them since the day after her death. He had taken them flowers to express what words could never express. They had shouted at him, hurled abuse and accusations. It was nothing he hadn't hurled at himself. He was used to it, so he had stood there numbly and accepted it all, tears rolling down his cheeks. There had been no point in trying to stop them; he felt guilty – he had killed his best friend. Alex heard the front door and shook his head. Tears were rolling down his cheeks again. He wiped them away angrily.

His mother was surprised to see him back so early, though it was already five o'clock. But she did not say anything about it and made his tea. Alex was in a thoughtful mood and couldn't get his mind off Jay. He ate his dinner mechanically and went to bed early, but that night he tossed and turned and was convinced the next day that he had not slept a wink. He hummed tunelessly as he prepared his lunch, partly because he was happy to be planning his revenge on Lilly-Rose for tattling to his mum and partly to banish the icy chill that he felt again.

Death grinned. He knew Revenge very well. They often helped each other in their devious plans. But Revenge, like Death, was a busy person, and getting together with him was always tricky. Death was very pleased that Alex had met his friend. It was their first encounter, so it was an important one. Revenge had to succeed today – but not completely! Revenge could give Alex that little something he needed.

At lunch time, Alex pulled out his flask. As usual, Lilly-Rose flounced over just to annoy him and asked if he could spare some of his juice. He knew that even if he said no, she would take some, so he said no. She was a very predictable girl: she picked up the flask and drank from it. She swallowed as much as she could at once and then set it down, nearly empty. A strange look crossed her face as she registered the bitter aftertaste, but it was too late now. Lilly-Rose quickly hid her disgust and smiled at her friends. She then apologised for taking so much and strolled off as his friends teased him for letting her.

"Wait," he whispered to them. "Just wait."

During class after lunch, Lilly-Rose had to make a presentation. As she stood up, she teetered and nearly fell over. Suddenly her eyes rolled and she grabbed her stomach. Summoning all her strength, she ran out of the door towards the toilets. Alex grinned; it seemed to have worked. He wondered if she would die of it. He thought not and suddenly questioned whether he actually wanted her to. A few minutes later, her blond curly hair tied back out of the way, Lilly-Rose came back in and asked to go home because she had been sick. The teacher wasn't very happy because Lilly-Rose had only just recovered from a bout of flu. Alex's nemesis put on her most innocent face and said that she was very sorry and that her flu must not be finished yet. The teacher considered this and, likely thinking about the risk of it spreading to the other children, sent her home. Alex's friends looked at him. He was smirking as discreetly as he could, and it was obvious to them that he was the cause of her malaise.

When the final bell rang, Alex went straight home. He planned to go back to school a few days later to see what had happened to Lilly-Rose, but he wasn't going back the next day. No! Alex was going to have fun.

2

A LEX STARTED THE day by courting death on his
favourite stretch of the road. He leapt around, passing
through the lines of traffic but always moved forward with the
flow so that he would end up where he wanted to be, whether
it was the flyover, the railway bridge, or anywhere else he
fancied. He'd never considered what would happen if a police
officer caught him. Would he be sent to prison? The thought
of prison excited him, and his adrenaline suddenly surged as
he sprang forward with more speed and courage. He might, of
course, just get taken back home, and then his parents would
find out about him playing truant. He had barely landed after
vaulting over the bonnet of a Citroën ZX when a car screeched
to a stop behind him. He threw himself out of the way and
cleared a bit more ground before turning back to look at the
car. It was stationary; the occupants had pulled onto the hard
shoulder and were consulting a map. He approached the car
cautiously, pulled by some unknown force. The driver peered
out of the window, frowned, and spoke to Alex.

"Say, what are you doing out by yourself?" Alex's
adrenaline rush left him then and there. The men appeared
serious and intimidating for some reason. Before he could
quite rationalise this fear, Alex had taken off, his body

reacting of its own accord. Prison, or being caught, didn't seem attractive after all!

Death was lying on his stomach on the roof of the car, waiting for the fun to happen. His head was propped up, and his eyes flicked from one place to the other. His legs were bent upwards at his knee, and he kicked them rhythmically like a child unable to hold still. He was not bored for the moment because he knew that his excitement was growing. He was ready to burst. At last Alex had met Fear ... Not that they were complete strangers, because Fear had been there to advise him on previous occasions, but Alex had so far proven quite uninterested in him. This was the beginning of something! Fear of man, fear of danger, but more importantly, fear of Death – that would be Death's ultimate goal.

After having left the A road soon after his strange experience, Alex had sat for a while on a bench in a park. He tried to explain to himself what had happened, what he had done, and even how he had arrived at that park and that bench. He could find no reason, no logic in what he had done. He wasn't even sure he knew where he was! He sat for a while, which was unusual for Alex, but then the need for adrenaline kicked in, and he started planning a petty theft, something he had never done before. He couldn't quite come to terms with that odd feeling and his reaction, which had seemed almost mechanical and illogical to him. Why had his reflexes kicked in and leapt away from the car and back into the traffic? He pondered these questions slowly as he made his way back to familiar territory.

Alex stood in a part of town he had often meandered through on school days. Nothing seemed to have changed since last week. There was the vegetable store Jim looked after, and there, right in the centre of the market place, was the stall he had chosen for his theft. It was a very expensive one, and he knew that his mother needed something from it that she could not afford. He strolled by and feigned interest in the fresh fish. He was actually looking for the item his mother needed. There it was: the most expensive thing in the stall.

As Alex planned his next move, his brain whizzed ahead to what would happen once he had stolen it. Would the police arrest him? Would they be able to catch him? If not, did they know who he was, and would they be able to track him down? Would it be worth it for him? He glanced back at Jim. He had not seen Alex. Maybe that was the way!

He ambled towards the vegetable store and waved cheerily at the short man in the apron. Although Alex was not supposed to know about Jim and his mum, he had seen them together a couple of times – aside from when he was hiding – and Jim had been introduced as "an old family friend". The two exchanged small talk, and Alex mentioned his teacher being ill as the reason for his not being in school. Whether he was believed or not was unimportant to Alex: he had quite a different agenda! He waved goodbye and walked a few stalls further down.

He looked around again; the market place was still bustling with people, and there were two policemen chatting with the man monitoring the cheese stall. Now that someone could identify him, it was safe to go ahead with his plan. He looked at the shopkeeper, who was busy with his long queue of customers. Alex made a dash for the much-wanted thing. His hand reached out and nearly grasped it when someone jostled him. His hand jerked in the other direction and found itself in an open handbag. The owner had not noticed, so he took out her purse and spun away from her. There was hardly any money inside, so he Alex turned back around and brazenly walked up to the lady, handed the purse to her, and walked away. The lady frowned at him suspiciously. He was walking towards the fish stall. She waved at one of the policemen standing near the cheese stall and drew Alex to his attention. He nodded patiently and glanced over in Alex's direction. Alex had made his way back to the queue and was waiting; he had decided to be as daring as he could. It was finally his turn to be served.

"Three jars of those olives, please."

The manager glanced behind him at the stuffed olives as Alex quickly crammed his pockets with little bags of spice and fled. He hadn't intended to take the spices; he had thought he had it in him to reach further, right to the man's cash box, but when the owner had turned his back, Alex had lost courage and grabbed what was the closest. Still, saffron wasn't that cheap! The man turned around with the jars, but Alex had gone. He shrugged and served his next customer. The customers were shocked at Alex's boldness but were too startled to stop him. Once he had run, however, they all shouted after him and called the police over.

The policeman had been watching Alex and threaded his way through the crowd to intercept him. Alex did not even look up but darted swiftly around him. The policeman called after him, and Alex broke into a sprint. The policeman waved to the other officers, and they united in an effort to corner Alex. He was a good runner – or so he had thought – but they easily caught him just round the bend in the road, and an officer took down his details and made him return the spices to the shop owner. Alex suddenly decided this wasn't what he had wanted. The planning, the adrenaline rush – oh yes! But not the rough handling and pushing and shoving, and not the boredom of sitting at the police station. This was more than he had bargained for.

Alex was not yet eighteen, so the police had to detain him until a parent or guardian came for him. They tried to contact his mother, but Alex had not given them the right address, so they could not. Boredom was beginning to set in for Alex. His eyes surveyed the room. They had not put him in a cell. They had just left him in an ordinary room with a guard who seemed to have other responsibilities. He left the room repeatedly and then came back in again sighing wearily. The guard walked out to answer a call, and Alex was on the point of standing up to see if he could leave without drawing attention to himself when a man entered and sat down opposite him. He was followed by Alex's father. Alex was shocked, but he quickly put two and two together and remembered having waved to Jim, who must have given Alex's details to the police when they canvassed for information at the market.

Alex's father was not in a mood to talk. He listened to the police officer's report; grunted at Alex to indicate that he should apologise and promise it would not happen again; signed the release form, then followed Alex out of the station, making sure he had Alex's arm tightly squeezed in his hand the whole time. Alex was not going to escape! The boy sighed; this was not quite what he had imagined. The adrenaline had lasted all of three minutes: the time between asking for the olives and running away from the stall. That had been it. But that other feeling – the emotion which had crushed him when he got caught – that was new. It was the same "buzz" that had made him leap away from that car. It was new and he couldn't identify it.

The quivering excitement of Death was something terrible to see. He was jumping up and down, his claws exposed as he held his breath. His eyes still gleamed and he was becoming increasingly agitated. The master plan had started! Any minute now, Alex would realise what it was … who it was. Death could hardly contain himself. His plan, his little project that he had worked on for so long, was finally coming to fruition. He dug his nails into his legs with impatience. Then suddenly he drew himself up short. The process had started, but only slowly – Alex could still not identify Fear!

"They caught him stealing!"

Alex's mother looked from him to his dad in disbelief. She was speechless for a while, just staring at him whilst his dad made himself a coffee and then headed back to work. Once he'd left, Alex's mum found her voice, and what a voice it was! Alex had not heard her speak in that tone and at that volume for a long time. Nothing he had done appeared to have had any effect on her for a long while, and his lies were never questioned. Suddenly it was like having his old mum back – the mum she was to him before Jim had disrupted their family. Jim? Or Jay's death – Alex shook Jay out of his mind. He mustn't think about her now; this wasn't her fault.

He sat in a daze, not listening to his mum, but not thinking anything either. Her complaint that they were not that poor suddenly rang out loud and clear, catching his attention. He looked over at her. She ordered him not to steal anymore or she would have to send him to a young offender's institution. Would she really do that? Could she? Not long ago he'd have jumped at the prospect, as he had at the idea of going to prison. Now however, after today, his enthusiasm had dwindled. He expressed his horror at the idea and looked remorseful. His mother assumed that would be the end of it and sent him up to his room.

He slumped on his bed, pulling the covers up under him to get comfortable. His mother would never understand the rush, the adrenaline, the excitement. She could not empathise if she wanted to! Alex remembered the first time he had played with matches and had watched some grass burn. His mind had suddenly visualised the whole garden burning, and he had laughed out loud as he imagined the leaves curling up and going brown, then red, in the heat. His mother had heard him through the kitchen window and come out smiling to ask what he was laughing about. Her smile had vanished and her eyes had widened as she saw the grass burning next to him. It had just been a small bit, nothing her garden hose hadn't been able to fizzle out in less than a couple of seconds. He had hurt nobody.

In response to her quizzing, Alex had explained what he had thought of, what he had longed to do if he had not been so young. She had calmly, but firmly, sent him to his room. He had gone quietly, but the fantasy had developed in secret, and he had often relived that afternoon in his dreams.

He closed his eyes and watched the garden burn again, but this time his imagination let him down. He opened his eyes again and sighed. He had no matches in his room; he could have played with some of his old textbooks ...

Dinner time came too fast. Alex's mum was in a funny mood, but then so was he. He couldn't seem to concentrate on anything. He couldn't relive the fire in the garden; he couldn't plan anything exciting; his thoughts wouldn't stay in one place; and he felt tired, drained. He slouched away to his room after dinner and didn't leave it again.

T HE NEXT DAY, Alex got up and went to school to show his mother that he wanted to be obedient. She took him there by car and left him in Neil's care. He told Neil what had happened the previous day and then left school. He did not feel like hanging around to speak to the teacher or get sent to the headmaster.

He went out to Lilly-Rose's house and paid her a call. She was in her pyjamas when she opened the door and looked very pale. She was astonished to see him there.

"Hi" he said, awkwardly. "I just popped by to see how you are." Alex realised he should never have come. Of course she hadn't died, and now, well, now she'd tell everyone he cared and had a crush on her. That would only lead to him getting more annoyed at all the silly attention she gave him.

"Hello, I'm okay, just a bit of indigestion. Thanks for coming to see me. Do you want to come in?!

He made an excuse then and left. He swore under his breath because the potion had not worked. He sat down on the edge of the flyover and started to think about something else for her to drink or eat.

Death was shocked. He stood as still as stone and as cold as ice. His plan to give Alex a reason to live was not working out at all! Fear had met Alex – there had been no reaction, or none worth speaking of. Now Lilly-Rose's affection for Alex was not working either. Death's big plan, which Mischief had helped him hatch, was in ruins. He sighed heavily and abandoned Alex for a time. Death would have to figure out something else!

Alex was surprisingly inactive all day and had a weird premonition that something positive was going to happen to him. If only he knew where he should wait for it, he would go there. As it was, he had not the foggiest idea of where to go, so he decided to do some queue jumping. He leapt in and out with the ease of practice, but suddenly he stopped. The next second a car zoomed up, but just before it hit him, he jumped out of the way. Lying in the gutter he pushed away the tears that were welling up in his eyes; he had nearly succeeded, but his instinct had "saved" him! He thought about Jay and pinched himself for letting his tears out. If only he had her reflexes, he would be dead by now.

Her face seemed to smile down at him. "Her reflexes" – had he really thought that? Alex had been impressed by her from the start: the vibrant smile and the confident attitude were lacking amongst his friends at school. But her reflexes had also been a reason they got on. He had taken her down past the motorway that first time and showed her what it was he did there. As he jumped, he'd been wondering why he was doing this, why he was showing a girl what he enjoyed doing. But before he realised it, she was there, in the traffic with him, running in between the cars and scaring the life out of both the drivers and him.

Alex stood up and brushed off his hands. He'd had enough of cars now. He made his way slowly to the bridge over the railway line.

Death was pacing in his cold, empty room, his clothes making a draft as he walked up and down, but there was nobody there to notice. He could still not get over his failure. He had never suffered from guilty feelings or remorse. His conscience had deserted him long ago. But now he was examining his motives for killing Jay before Alex. He could have killed Alex first and then Jay. He was suffering from the annoyance of knowing that he would not be able to triumph in Alex's death because Alex wanted it himself. His grand plan had failed miserably. Alex should have recognised Fear when they had met, then fallen for Lilly-Rose – that had been the spice in Death's dreams for the past while. But now there would be no feast to invite his colleagues to, no big celebrations as there had been for Jay. He felt depressed. After much thought and anger he suddenly realised there might still be a way. It was not his fault after all. His henchman was to blame; Mischief had failed. Death needed only to find another, more effective aide to help him!

Alex walked along the railway tracks backwards, swaying this way and that and very often falling off. He was not seeking Death at the moment; he was just having fun. Suddenly, there was a loud whistle from around the corner. He did not move. A train was coming! Death was hurtling towards him! Would it work? He closed his eyes in an attempt to subdue his natural reflex to jump off the track as the train came nearer, but nothing happened. There was no trembling of rails, no rumbling of carriages, no squeaking of brakes, and the whistle suddenly stopped too. He could hear nothing now!

He opened his eyes and saw a wiry girl running towards him. When she noticed him looking at her, she began screeching and blowing on a whistle. She came to a halt directly in front of him and glared defiantly. She reminded him of Jay. Jay had been the first and only person he had taken along the ditch beside the busiest road he used – the only other person he'd ever taken to his island and the only person he'd ever seen on the tracks. Now this girl was here standing awkwardly before him. He stared back and then offered her a wary smile and greeting: "Hi".

She seemed taken aback, unsure of how to react. She was obviously surprised there was someone else on her tracks. Her eyes looked him up and down, sizing him up. Alex did the same. They could be friends, enemies, or strangers, but he liked the look of her. Finally she softened.

"Run with me," was all she said. Alex nodded, and they set off running down the track. When they saw the train coming in the distance, the girl jumped off the tracks and skipped to the edge of the bank. She stood there, looking victorious for a minute before realising that he had stayed. A horrified look crossed her face as she sprinted back to him and pulled him off. They were thrown over by the rush of the train, and Alex found himself lying next to her, not dead! He got up and helped her to her feet. She looked at him with astonishment written all over her face. He had not even thanked her!

"You could thank me." She said curtly, starting to wonder whether she had done the right thing.

Alex shrugged half-heartedly and glanced at her, she looked upset. But why should he care. He sighed.

"Thanks."

The girl's face was now like stone, and he realised he h.
no idea what she was thinking. It was as though she cou
block her face from expressing anything.

Alex took a step back and scrutinised the girl thoroughl
A few minutes ago he had been alone on the tracks, somewher
deep in his own consciousness. Then she had appeared, out
of nowhere. Her face was unreadable. She was tall, probably
about his age, maybe slightly younger. Her freckled nose
suddenly twitched, and he realised he had been staring for
quite a while. Her expression had changed now, and she was
obviously expecting an explanation. He blurted out that he
wanted to die but could never manage to.

He almost told her why. He stopped himself just in time.
Who was she exactly? And who was she to him? Why would
he tell her something he had never told anyone? Not even Jay's
parents knew what had actually happened. He had not been
able to visit them to explain, not after that horrible day. After
they had accused Alex of murdering her, he could not bring
himself to speak to them or go near them. They had never
known the extent of his relationship with Jay. They would
never know how much she had meant to Alex.

Since the day he had met her, Jay had been his reason for
living, his sole purpose. He ran for Jay, he woke up for Jay, he
skipped classes for Jay. Jay was Monday, Tuesday, Wednesday,
and Thursday for him – that is, she had been. She had been
Friday, Saturday, and Sunday too – his whole world! She had
been the reason he had not died so many times, leaping out
of the way of Death with a surge of adrenalin. Until … His
eyes blinked, and he realised he had not been telling the girl
this – he had been thinking it.

He sighed. All of that was still locked up inside him. He had never told anyone that he wanted to die, that he needed to die. He wanted to find Jay! The new girl was watching him intently. Her question remained unanswered, but she didn't ask again. She stepped boldly towards him, staring at him quizzically and then backed off and sat on the grass in silence. Alex looked at her and wondered, what was it about her that reminded him of Jay? Why was there a sudden peace within him? Had he believed in reincarnation, he would probably have decided she was Jay. The girl wanted to live dangerously, like he used to. Could he give in to his first instinct and open up to her? He would somehow have to make room for her in his life.

She did not look that much like Jay; she had shoulder-length red hair and green eyes. She was wearing purple jeans and braces, yellow braces! He looked her up and down again with sudden disdain; she was totally unlike Jay, and nothing and no one would ever make him forget her – and certainly not replace her. She was a stupid girl to imagine that he could let her be a part of his life just like that – and assuming she could make him want to live! To forget Jay – unthinkable! He shook his head and turned his back on her. No more girls for him. Jay was the first and last one he would ever let into his life. Alex stomped away, trying to justify his thoughts to himself. The girl had never actually asked to become part of his life, nor had she mentioned giving him the desire to live again, but surely her face had said it all. Or had it? He felt very confused all of a sudden.

Death stared down at Alex. Why was he doing this? Why was he turning away someone who could give him back the joy of living? Was he mad? Death covered his face in despair and then peeped out from between his fingers. Alex was walking proudly away, and the girl was just sitting there, staring at him. Death scowled and ran his fingers through his jet-black hair. He had been thinking of adding red streaks – to celebrate Alex's decision. Well, that plan must be deferred. Killing people who wanted to die was not something he enjoyed, but maybe, this once, he would just have to do it.

Alex looked over his shoulder as he neared the corner. He was hoping for another glimpse of the girl, but she was gone. She had not seemed concerned that he had been so rude; she certainly did not care. Part of him wanted to go home, but it was too early, so he decided to go back to race the cars. In future, he would stay there and not venture out to the train tracks anymore. He did not want to meet up with this presumptuous girl again, especially as he had a feeling that he did not despise her as much as he wanted to.

However, the next morning, he woke up with a yearning to go and find the girl and apologise to her. Of course she could help him forget Jay; was he not looking for that very thing? Well, either that or Death. He hardened his heart and ordered himself to ignore his desire to apologise. He made himself get out of bed slowly and get dressed even more slowly. As he pulled a black T-shirt over his head, his thoughts strayed. What could her name be? Where was she from, and how come he'd never seen her before? He shook his head. No. He wouldn't give in! So what would he do today? He was definitely not going down to the railway tracks. He repeated this three times out loud to himself, and just when he thought that he had mastered his yearning to go there, it bounced back and hit him full in the face. Drat her, that girl – she was not going to take his railway away from him! No one had the right to do that to him, and she would not change anything about him. If he met her, he could certainly ignore her. He laced up his shoes on his doorstep, looking down the road towards the motorway.

There was a light fog, which made the queue-jumping even more dangerous, and he loved it! He decided that he would race the cars all the way to the train so that he did not have to go there by the less exciting way. He popped back into the kitchen, grabbed his lunch, shoved it into a carrier bag, and ran out the front door. His mother looked after him disapprovingly but then shrugged her shoulders. She knew he was not going to school, but as long as he did not get hurt and did not get home before half past four, there was no problem. Her pep talk after his petty theft had been a one-off; she had not reverted to the mum she had once been. Alex had realised shortly after that incident that it was not Jim who had caused his mother to change: it was he, himself, or rather, him and Jay.

Alex had been close to his mum as he grew up. He was an only child and had found out quite young that his parents had wanted him to have a sibling, but it hadn't worked out. As a toddler, his mum took him everywhere and did everything with him. Once he started school, she had carried on looking after him and being a great parent, or so he thought now, in hindsight. Then he had turned into a rebellious teen, and her words had no longer had an impact on him, or so he liked to think. The reality of it was that he'd listen to her, and do his best, but his adrenaline addiction was too strong for him to stop his habits. And then Jay had appeared on the scene.

She had replaced the friendship he'd had with his mum, and they had all accepted it. When Jay had left them – that, he realised now, had been the breaking point. He had no more relationship with his mother. Two years of silence had taken their toll, and she didn't know how to be there for him, or he for her.

Alex had reached the road he had chosen now, and, as usual, he silenced all his thoughts and concentrated. He leapt out over the bonnet of a Skoda and landed just in front of a Mercedes that braked suddenly. The driver leant out of his window and started yelling. Alex ran along between the two cars, listening to the drivers' shouts, and then he lost them by vaulting over the Mercedes' boot and landing next to another Mercedes. This one had a trailer, and for some reason he made the unusual decision to get into it and not continue upsetting the drivers. It was weird. None of the drivers knew him; he was out there every morning at a similar time, but he never stayed on that stretch of the road for long, and he tried to pick a different place to play each day. People hurled insults at him; some spoke decently to him on occasion. Others ignored him, gave him a wide berth, or honked their horns at him energetically. Some of the drivers, on the slower roads, tried to get his surname and address, but he never gave it despite their cajoling. He figured the police would cause him more hassle for this than for stealing.

Stealing could not get you killed. The buzz from stealing was neither as intense nor as long-lived as the one derived from car-hopping. Stealing was not something he wanted to do every day. His dabble in pilfering and visiting the police station had been enough for him.

Finally the car Alex rode was in sight of the bridge that went over the tracks, and Alex leapt out onto the pavement. He surprised himself by waiting patiently for the cars to stop before stepping out into the road and by using the zebra crossing. Any other day, he would not even have thought of it. He climbed down the steep bank and stepped onto the tracks, wobbled once, and then found his balance again. He wondered if he would see the girl; he hoped he would, even if he ignored her. He was suddenly angry at her for invading his thoughts again. If only he could hurt her. Yes, that was it, he had to hurt her. That would teach her a lesson.

Suddenly, he was bowled over and found himself lying face down on the tracks, the wind knocked out of him. He heard a piercing whistle. He jumped up indignantly. It was the girl, of course; it had to be. What cheek she had to run at him and knock him over, and she had not even stopped to see if he was all right! He would pay her back! He could still hear her whistle, so he knew that he could catch her up. He pelted down the track and around the corner. She was there, running at full speed and whistling. He ran flat out, decreasing the distance between them, and when he caught her up, he grabbed at her roughly and spun her round to face him. Expressionless, she looked into his furious eyes. He was still reeling from having been bowled over, but her face again betrayed no emotion.

"What do you think you are doing?" he asked her, still outraged.

"You want the train to kill you, don't you? I'm the train, and I've knocked you over! You're supposed to be dead!"

Her face relaxed suddenly, and Alex could see she was studying his reaction. She shook her arm free but carried on watching him. Alex was not amused, but her face unsettled him and he didn't know how to feel. She was strong, confident, decisive; she didn't need him, and he didn't need her, and yet here they both were, seeking each other out.

Alex hesitated. He had caught her up, promised himself he'd pay her back ... Now what? Alex groaned silently, unsure himself of what to do next. Taking advantage of his indecision, she bolted. He pursued her. Boy, could she run fast! He finally drew level with her and wrestled her down onto the wooden sleepers and kept her there by sitting on her. He was the victor! She had merely pushed him over, taken him by surprise, but he could keep her down. She wriggled and squirmed and managed to get her arms free, but, push and scratch as she may, she still could not get him off her. Then a whistle sounded, and the rails started to tremble. The girl's eyes widened, and she pleaded for him to release her. He stood up and she leapt after him. In a flash she was on the grass verge, grabbing at his hand as he let her pull him off the tracks. The train whizzed by at an amazing speed and soon was gone. Alex stood and watched it wistfully. The girl stood there and looked at him sadly.

Death smiled. He could see that Alex was getting used to his new companion, but he doubted that they would ever get together. But then, that was not a problem: Cupid would be more than happy to help him on that one, just as long as Death's real intentions weren't obvious. Maybe this was why he hadn't thought of Cupid previously – because Lilly-Rose wasn't the right girl for Alex. Or maybe it was just that Cupid was insufferably sweet, and Death couldn't stand him. He peered down again and watched the two standing awkwardly, looking at each other, not sure of what to say. As long as Alex's death wish disappeared, Death reasoned to himself, it did not really matter if they got together or not. Alex's desire to live must be rekindled. Then Death could be victorious!

Alex looked at the girl, and she looked back. Unconsciously, they both knew that they were neither enemies nor strangers. Alex had accepted her unspoken suggestion. This meant a great deal to him. He would have to get used to company again. He was not yet completely at ease with her, but he'd give it some time. As they ran in silence down the track, Alex felt like he was watching them objectively from above. He could see them both running; they were so alike: bold, proud, and stubborn. He acknowledged that he felt relieved, as though a weight had been lifted off him. They stopped at last, out of breath. They stepped off the tracks together and flung themselves onto the bank, gasping.

Alex wanted to talk. He wanted to tell her. All those secrets shared with Jay were finally going to come bursting out. This girl needed to know how much Jay had meant to him and what their relationship had been like. She needed to know what she was up against. The adrenaline, the silences, the running, the dares. He glanced over at her. She was sitting next to him, perhaps lost in her own dark thoughts. Maybe she also had a story to tell. Why she was here? Why she was not in school? His thoughts wandered away, and the urge to talk about Jay subsided – the moment had passed.

He went home that day feeling exceedingly happy and with a meeting set for the next day. He kissed his mother as he went through the kitchen and did not slam the door behind him. His mother was astonished, but she did not say anything; she knew she had lost the right to question him. He hummed all the way up to his room and actually came back down to ask when tea would be ready instead of shouting from upstairs. His mum started to worry because she had some bad news and did not want to spoil Alex's sudden good mood. She decided that she would tell him over tea because he would ask why she wasn't waiting for his dad to eat with them anyway. When she called him down to tea, he came down noiselessly and slipped into his seat. He said not a word and did not ask why his father wasn't there. She wondered whether he was aware that something was wrong. She sat down opposite him and cut her bread. She hesitated and then put her knife down. She took a deep breath and opened her mouth to speak. Alex opened his too and interrupted her.

"I know. He left a note. On my bed."

She stared at him. She politely but rather coldly inquired to see what it said. Alex left his roll untouched: never talk with your mouth full.

"It explained everything very well," he said. "It's all your fault. Dad said he'd had enough. He said you were cheating on him and that he was leaving. There wasn't much to the note. He said 'bye' and that he'd see me sometime."

He looked up at his mother. There were tears in her eyes, but he could not understand why. She knew it was her fault. The whole neighbourhood knew about her affairs. His dad had probably known for a long time. Maybe it was because of Alex she was crying. Was he going to live with his dad? What a scary prospect!

They continued to eat in silence until Alex dared to ask what would happen to him. His mum looked up, very ashamed of herself. In fact she had suggested to his father that he take Alex, for she had no wish to have him around the house, but his father had refused so she had to keep him. She didn't want to inflict further pain on Alex, so she lied: she told Alex that she wanted him to live with her, but that one weekend a month, he could go to see his father if he liked.

The arrangement suited Alex. It meant that while he was at his mother's he was free to do as he pleased during the day because she would not know and that at night he could slip out without her noticing, for she would be busy. He wondered, briefly, whether he would ever see his dad again. He somehow wished he could say goodbye. Then again he thought, reasoning all emotion out of his heart, they did not see eye to eye anyway. His dad had probably not wanted him.

Death was no longer despairing. Alex had paired up with the only person Death knew of who could make him forget Jay! Soon he would be very keen to live. All of Death's past excitement was resurging. He thought gleefully of ways to kill them. He would, of course, have to kill both of them; otherwise, he would not be able to kill the girl at all. Last time he had only killed the one, and he was still regretting it. This boded well; he could have a double feast or even celebrate twice separately, and everyone would come and congratulate him. Yes, Death was gleefully looking forward to the future – and he immediately started planning what he would wear to the party.

Alex went to bed early that night, hoping to be up early the next day, but he lay awake a long time, thinking. He was still comparing Jay to this new girl and noticing the differences. He then realised that he still did not know her name and that he had not told her his either. He tried suitable names on her picture in his imagination. Kim seemed to fit very well, but there was something that wasn't quite right in it. Mel, short for Melody. It fit much better that Kim did, but Alex found that Jim suited her even better. He soon realised that even Michael or Ben suited her better than Kim. Why was it that she was more like a boy than a girl? Jay had been like that too, but feminine names like Isabella or Chloe had suited her too. He fell asleep dreaming of Jay's beautiful black hair that was tinted here and there with the same red as the unnamed girl's.

He woke up with a stiff back and was reluctant to get up, but as soon as he remembered his date, he was out of bed and into the shower in a flash. He threw on some clean clothes and gobbled his breakfast. He kissed his mother before running out of the house and down to the motorway, where he threw his bag off his back and settled down to wait for the girl. She arrived later than they had agreed upon, but she made no mention of it. "Hey" was all she said, with a curt nod at him. He replied in the same way, realising all of a sudden that they had spent the previous day in silence, but his chaotic thoughts had made up for the lack of conversation.

He stood up slowly, reluctant to look as if he had been eagerly waiting to see her again. She stood awkwardly but stared at him unflinchingly and asked him his name. He grinned, an impulsive grin that later on he could not explain, and told her. She was called Maxine. That was it! He had been right: Max – short for Maxine. He had known she would have a boy's name! They ran along the side of the motorway separately until they came to the bridge that passed over the railroad tracks. Maxine stopped, peered over it, and then looked back over her shoulder and raised her eyebrows questioningly. Alex leapt through a few lanes of traffic and came to a standstill next to her.

"Can you climb down the bridge?" Maxine asked.

Alex stared at her. This was something that even Jay wouldn't have thought of! He peered over and shivered. How would they do it? As he straightened up, Max's leg went over the edge, and down she went. Alex followed. It was easier than he had expected because the bricks were worn away in places and provided foot- and handholds for them. As he climbed down, he heard Max's foot slip, and his adrenaline started pumping. He couldn't look down to see if she was okay, but he stopped and listened. He could hear her somewhere below him – she had not fallen.

When he got to the bottom, he flopped down beside her on the grassy bank to catch his breath. Alex noticed the brambles close to him and rolled over and over till he was lying next to them, picking the blackberries off one by one. They were delicious. This was probably the best spot to come picking, somewhere nobody else could get to. He closed his eyes and stretched. Max sat up and prodded him in the ribs. He jumped, startled, and made a grab for her, but she slipped out of his grasp. He picked a few blackberries and threw them after her before chasing her down the sleepers. He caught up with her further along the track and debated with himself whether to push her off it and tackle her to the ground or just overtake her, challenging her to catch him.

As Alex got within reach, Max suddenly stopped, and Alex pounced on her. They rolled over off the tracks and down the embankment, where she struggled for a few minutes, trying unsuccessfully to throw him off her. She finally gave up and lay stiffly, refusing to look at him. He held her down victoriously for a few minutes, expecting her to acknowledge he'd won. But as Alex glanced down at her, he noticed that her face, which had once been unreadable, was now looking embarrassed.

He let her go, ashamed, and told her that she was a fast runner and that she was strong too. Her face relaxed a bit but didn't seem much happier. Alex got up, feeling odd, and ran off down the track; Max followed. The whirlwind in Alex's head was raging; emotions and hormones were twisted as in a cyclone, and all he could think about was Max. He'd only been playing, and yet, as he'd pinned her down and had fancied kissing her, her embarrassed, averted eyes had deterred him. It hadn't extinguished his desire, but he had known he couldn't; she was not to be touched.

By midday, Alex was exhausted as never before, so they threw themselves down in the ditch to rest. He reflected as he lay there. Max was odd. Her behaviour often reminded him of Jay, and yet he couldn't pinpoint what the likeness was. Jay had been an open book with him from day one: Max was closed, expressionless, and proud – much like he had now become. Maybe she had something she needed to share, something to get off her chest. He lay there watching her. Her head was slightly turned to one side, but he could hear her sighs and could see the tears rolling silently down her cheek. He was puzzled. Had it been Jay, he would have offered a hug – but this was Maxine and he hardly knew her. He reached out his hand and put it over hers ever so lightly. That expression from earlier was haunting him. Max stiffened for a second and then relaxed, but she wouldn't turn her head towards him and her hand slowly slipped out from under his.

Alex removed his hand as he wondered whether or not he could trust her. She sat up and turned to face him, tears now streaming down her face. There was an angry, resentful look in her eyes, as though she blamed Alex for making her cry. He reached out to pull her towards him, but she pushed him away roughly and stood up.

"I'm fine ... Sorry, life's hard at the moment," she said, and she turned away, scrubbing away her tears. She seemed ready to move on, so Alex caught her sleeve and told her his idea. Max did not know about Jay, not yet. But Alex could not bring himself to tell her. Each time he had felt the need to get rid of the heaviness hanging over him, every time he had felt it was all about to come boiling up, he had not been able to say anything. Alex knew that taking Maxine to the place that had been his and Jay's would be an easier way to do it. He didn't quite know how to suggest it, so he just blurted out, "I want to take you to a special place."

Alex almost immediately regretted it. This wouldn't work. How could he take anyone else to Jay's place? But it was too late now, and he did feel relieved. Max looked surprised and still very upset, but she agreed to go; they fell into step together in silence. Their hands swung next to each other, but Alex didn't dare take hers in his. He sensed she wouldn't let him.

Death's mouth fell open as he watched the events unfold under his nose. Alex was taking Maxine to the place where Death had met Jay, the morning of her delicious accident! He did not even need to help them; they were doing the work all by themselves. He could see that Alex was in anguish about the Maxine versus Jay problem, and he commanded Torment to increase the pressure.

Alex could not talk on the way there. He could not run or chase Maxine. She darted sideways glances at him the whole way, her face still reflecting some painful memory of her own. She tried asking him where it was they were going, but Alex couldn't find the words to answer. She was silent after that and sank into her own thoughts. She had not expected this. In fact, she had been struggling with her own life so much that she hadn't noticed that Alex was having a hard time. He had merely been a distraction for her, someone to spend time with during the long lonely days. She suddenly realised that he was going to share what he was struggling with. She shivered and wondered how he'd expect her to react.

Alex's mind was racing. His heart was full of the emotions that he had determined to push far out of his mind a couple of years ago. All of his excitement at seeing Jay again that final morning was forcing itself into his consciousness. He remembered what lunch he had packed. He recalled that, for the first time, they had agreed to meet in "their spot" instead of down by the tracks or on the roadside. In his mind's eye he saw the way they had walked – and chatted when they had got there.

Previous to the fateful day, they had always met up in a place of action and leapt straight into the traffic or onto the tracks; they had spared no time for anything else. But that was the day their relationship had changed from simple superficiality of actions to a deeper sharing of soul, wishes, hopes, and dreams. Jay had told him about her parents and why the family had moved to town. She was an only child, and her education was all that mattered to them. They hadn't consulted her about whether she wanted to move towns, schools, and classes, and all of a sudden she had been uprooted from friends, familiar routines, and security. Alex had marvelled at how well she seemed to have adapted – but then, she had only been to school half the time. He had wondered how she had managed to play truant so much without her parents finding out, but she had slipped into a silent reverie at that point. He had so many memories of that horrid day!

When Max and Alex arrived at the drainpipe, Alex stopped. He could go no further. Maxine stopped too and reached awkwardly for his hand, encouragingly. She wanted to know what this place was, and, although she was struggling too, she did not want him to feel rejected. Alex stood there with his eyes closed, memories of Jay assailing his senses.

The first time he had shown her his "hideout," Jay had been very serious. He had promised her that she could see it the next day, so she had dressed up specially. She had worn very wide army pants and a close-fitting top with a loose sleeveless cardigan wide open over it. He had thought her very pretty but had not dared to say so, and so she had never known. Together, they had crossed the bridge quietly and had lain down on the other side on a blanket of dry leaves under a weeping willow. Staring up at the swaying branches, Alex had finally divulged his story about his dad, his mum, her lover, and most of all, his addiction to adrenaline. This was one thing he had no explanation for, and yet this was what made him run on a daily basis. Jay had listened and cried with him, or for him, as he was unable to shed tears. She had given him a hug too, which had been awkward and had shifted the mood. Struggling out of her embrace, he had taken her on a tour of the island, and then they had set off to the motorway. If only he had known. He would have held her in his arms forever, ignoring the awkwardness, in order to prevent her from leaving him.

There would be no tenderness with Max today, though, he determined, glancing at her briefly. Unless she offered it first! They picked their way across the drainpipe and ambled around the island, slowly making their way towards the weeping willow tree. There were still bits of litter here and there, remains of the summer picnic parties. Alex stopped to pick them up as he passed by. Then they got to the middle of the island, and he paused in front of a curtain of weeping willow branches. He pulled them aside and motioned for Max to go into the shelter. There was a bag hanging from one of the trees, and he stepped over to put the rubbish in it.

Max looked around and was intrigued. She could feel the presence of someone else: a girl. She had a definite impression of what the girl was like and how close the relationship between her and Alex had been. Max felt sorrow for him and a growing curiosity to know who the girl was – and what had happened. She felt oddly apprehensive about her own emotions.

Alex stuffed the rubbish into the bag and turned slowly to gauge Maxine's reaction. She had her back to him, and she was sniffling and holding a tissue up to her eyes. He instinctively turned her around and hugged her to him, as if she were Jay.

"This is the first time that anyone's shared something so special with me," Max whispered.

Alex shivered. An odd feeling of déjà vu swept over him. He dropped his arms abruptly. He had decided that he wouldn't touch her, so why the sudden hug? She still did not know why he had really brought her here. She just thought this was a special place – she did not know about Jay.

Or did she? Alex knew the rumours that ran riot around his school about him and Jay. There had been rumours even before her death, but they had both been untouched by them. They had known where they stood with each other; there had been no awkwardness in their relationship. After Jay had died, all kinds of whispers had started about her murder, his motives, their "real" reason for truancy, and once he had even heard someone suggest that Jay had been pregnant. He'd never paid much attention to these either, but now he wondered whether Max had heard anything about him at whatever school she went to – when she went.

Maxine knew that Alex had led her into a wonderland – a place she could only dream of living in. It was a perfect island. Although the weeds were knee high and the ground was laden with dead leaves, she found it mysterious and beautiful. She turned her gaze on Alex, who had stepped away from her and walked to the tree trunk, collecting cigarette butts and rubbish as he went. He had a bin bag in one hand and some dry leaves in the other. She crunched over to him and joined him in pulling up weeds. Alex came back to reality with a jerk, smiled his thanks at her, and went on slowly, gathering up handfuls of leaves and empty coke cans. They cleared the area for an hour, and then Alex suddenly stopped. He was feeling increasingly anxious about what he needed to say to her and weary with trying to find words that would not scare her away.

"Max … I brought you here … This is my special place; this is where, this is …" Alex stammered. He could not get his words out smoothly; he could not say what he meant to, but he knew he had to. "I brought Jay here. This is where we met on the day … when, the morning she … went." He could not utter the word "died."

He fell silent, hoping for a response. After a few moments he stood up dejectedly and set himself to picking up the leaves and the litter again.

Maxine had sat down next to him when he had begun to speak, and now she stayed where she was, immobile. "There must be more," she thought. Jay, whoever that was, could not have just "gone" as Alex had said. So Max held her peace whilst she waited and watched and ruminated. Alex was a combination of such extremes: a strong adrenaline junkie yet so tortured with self-examination and silent introversion …

Alex was still picking bits and pieces up from the ground and uncovering little sprouts of greenery. He enjoyed doing this: it was therapeutic. There was no rush to it; adrenaline did not race through his body like it did every other second of the day. Maybe that was it. Maybe that was why he enjoyed it so much – it was so like Jay. Her interior calmness had seemed to exude from her in spite of everything else she did. He picked a few more spots clean and found the remains of the tulips he had planted after Jay … He had left the funeral early. As soon as they had lowered her coffin into the ground, he had broken away from the crowd. Her parents had not wanted him there and had frowned at his every move. He had not stayed to plant his tulip bulbs on her grave; he had instead gone back to the island and planted them there, close to his tree – to their tree.

He broke the silence, his back still turned to Maxine. "We had been friends for a year. A year and a bit. She ran with me," he said, haltingly. "She matched my speed. She chased cars. We spotted number plates whilst running, and we dared each other to do things … We never climbed down that bridge, though." He turned and looked at Maxine. She was watching with compassion, listening intently. She looked somehow different; her face was readable – she seemed on the verge of tears but was holding them back. He resisted his impulse to hug her. If only she were Jay, he thought.

"We met here on her last day. We crept across the pipe alone for the first time. We'd always met elsewhere and then come here later, but that day we made our own way to the tree. The island was mine. After I showed it to her, she made this place hers. She would make sure that everything within the curtains of the tree was clean and tidy. She loved it and cleared up every day, any rubbish, anything she did not like the look of. She even planted some flowers once."

Alex motioned towards Maxine's right, and she looked in that direction. She could partly make out something but was not quite sure what it was. She stood up, unsure of whether he wanted her to have a look or not. He seemed uncertain too. Max held her hand out to him, and they both went to what had been Jay's flower patch. The flowers had died. The brown, dry stalks were sticking up where they had been planted. But in the corner of the patch there was one orange primrose that seemed to have survived long after it should have wilted. Max indicated that one and smiled. Alex stared blankly into space. He was not seeing the flower, she realised: he was in his own world. He was standing there with Jay.

Maxine coughed quietly. It had been a very long while since Alex had last moved or spoken. His hand was squeezing hers harder and tighter, but he seemed not to realise he was still holding it. She glanced at her watch. It had only been ten minutes, she realised. Alex grimaced.

"I remember every detail. I wish I didn't! We slipped across the pipe, each of us alone, and met here. Jay had been here for a while when I arrived. She had made it look perfect. The leaves were arranged beautifully, in a smooth blanket, covering the roots of the trees." He stopped, replaying what he had just said. He sounded like an idiot. Did he really take in all of that on that day? Had Jay known what was going to happen? It had all been too perfect!

Alex abruptly cut his story short. He was suddenly overwhelmed with embarrassment over everything he had just said. He had poured out his soul to a girl! A girl he had only met a brief while ago!

"She died," he said curtly. Then throwing the bag down, he said he had to go home to his mum. Maxine looked at him, surprised. He had not finished the story. She was curious and wanted to know more, but his face said it all: leave me alone. So she accompanied him to the drainpipe and asked at what time they should meet the next day. He looked at her blankly for a moment; then he shrugged and started crossing. They ran to the motorway to collect their bags, Alex trying to outrace her to avoid questions and Max intentionally lagging behind in a very confused state of mind.

Alex walked home in a bad mood. He liked Maxine, and if he had not told her his soppy story about Jay, he would have loved to see her again. As it was now, he was too embarrassed.

Death drummed his fingers on the table. He had another few sleepless nights to wait, and then he would be partially satisfied. He was getting impatient, but he knew that the longer the delay seemed to Alex, the more he would want to see Maxine, so Death did nothing. He was inspecting his newly filed fingernails when

There was a rhythmic knock on the door and Mischief barged in explaining that he wouldn't be able to sleep either so they could "not sleep" together. Death was not altogether impressed. He had blamed his previous failure on his friend and had coerced Cupid to help out this time instead. But Mischief did have a small part in the next day's mission. Death decided to let him stay so they could review their strategy. Death couldn't afford to fail this time!

4

ALEX WOKE UP very early the following day, and he slipped out before his mother was up, taking a few peanut butter sandwiches with him. He ran all the way down to the motorway and then stopped suddenly. There, in front of him, facing the other way, was Maxine. He hesitated. Should he go to her or should he hide until she went away? The moment of hesitation was his downfall because she turned around and spied him. She ran up to him, expectantly, with a half smile and asked if he would go to the train tracks with her. He sighed. He really wanted to spend time with her, but he was embarrassed. He refused curtly and started off the other way.

She shrugged angrily, despising herself for caring, and leapt out into the stream of passing cars. Alex swivelled round when he heard the horns and screeching brakes, and smiled wistfully at her wiry figure leaping around, frustrating the drivers. He then turned his head to inspect the cars that were driving past him. On a normal day he'd have been out there dancing through the traffic, probably before Maxine had had time to turn and see him ... Today was different; he couldn't focus on the cars, their speed, and his angle. Instead he just stared at them.

There were lots of jeeps, and the majority of the cars were black. There were also vast quantities of Renaults. A huge Porsche with darkened windows drove past extremely slowly, considering it was an A road. Normally Alex would have leapt at the opportunity to bait the driver. A slow-moving massive car was perfect to warm up with. But not today. Today he was feeling like a baby. He wanted to sit and cry, to hide and feel sorry for himself. He so wished he had not said anything to Max. He glanced around again hopefully – but she had gone. Had she been there, he might have run after her, but it was too late.

He walked slowly along the edge of the road, scuffing his shoes and berating himself for his indecisiveness, wishing somehow that the death wish were back. What was the point of today? He could not see Maxine; he was too proud to go and seek her out. He could not go home; what would he do with his mother all day? Where could he go? He suddenly realised how empty and lonely he really was.

Right after Jay had died, he had felt alone a couple of times. He had found himself searching for her and wondering irrationally if she might return. Over time he had got used to being alone and had started feeling confident in his independence. But now the unexpected weight of the same loneliness threatened to crush him.

Death smiled. Mischief had done well today, bringing the teenagers together "by chance" at the motorway. It had definitely showed Alex that he felt something for Maxine! Death would ruin them both at once! This had been his plan all along, but now he could start seeing the fruit of his labours. Alex's sudden lack of interest in being alone, in courting Death at every turn, at

*daring Death to conquer him, this was what he had been waiting
for. Now it was time! Now was the moment! Now all Death had
to do was to find a thrilling way of killing off Alex and Maxine.
Mischief smiled, accepting Death's praise, and then slid out of
the room. He didn't need to steal the limelight; he had other fish
to fry.*

Alex slunk down to the train tracks, hoping to see
Maxine and somehow shrug off his embarrassment. He could
"accidentally" bump into her again down there and could say
he had finished his errands for the day. Maybe he could even
spend the rest of the daylight hours with her, but he couldn't
spot her. He turned reluctantly to leave, but a flash of bright
pink in the bushes caught his eye; it was Maxine's bag. He
threw himself down beside it and waited for her.

He got out his sandwiches and munched on them in
silence. What was wrong with him? He couldn't remember
a time when he had sat still, alone – not since Jay had gone –
or the other day on the island. He spent most of his time
running from some kind of danger, daring that peril to come
and get him. And yet here he was, waiting for a girl, waiting
for Maxine.

He fell asleep after lunch as the hours dragged on and
she didn't appear. When he awoke, it was early evening and
shadows were lengthening. He hid in the bushes to play a trick
on her, hoping she would soon return. He laughed silently,
in anticipation of the shock that he would give his friend.
Presently she sauntered along, and, as she grabbed her bag,
he jumped out at her, hooting scarily. She jumped backwards
as he reached for her; then she slapped him sharply, but he
could not stop giggling. He could see she was trembling and

realised that he had really frightened her, but he still could not stop laughing.

Finally, after a few apologies, Maxine agreed that no harm was done and perhaps it was funny, and they walked back together, towards his home. He noticed that she let him walk much closer than she had done up till then. She was still quivering from the shock, and he could feel the slight tremors of her arm the whole way home. On arriving at his doorstep, they went their separate ways, happy to be friends again and promising to get together early the next day. Alex went inside with the taste of laughter on his lips.

He went straight upstairs to his room. He wasn't hungry, and he needed some blank wall space to stare at. The thoughts in his head no longer made any sense to him; it was becoming too crowded up there. He sat and analysed his day: no adrenaline, no need for it, his desire to see Maxine, her proximity, and her fear. Why had his harmless joke scared her so much? She was an adrenaline junkie like he was. She lived outdoors … or wait, where did she live? He stretched out on his bed and closed his eyes. Soon he was fast asleep, and his subconscious was left to sort itself out alone.

Morning light came more quickly than he had expected but more slowly than he had wanted. He yawned and stretched. He cracked his back a few times, bending over backwards to do so, threw on some clothes, and ran downstairs. His mother gave him some sandwiches, and he ran out the front door. He stopped in his tracks. There on the other side of the road was Maxine. They had arranged to meet down at the railway line. Alex glanced over his shoulder, and he could see his mother watching him through the lounge window. Maxine darted across the road and grabbed his hand eagerly.

"Are you ready?" she asked in an excited voice.

Alex was not so sure. Now what would he tell his mother? She would be nagging at him forever about being too young to have a girlfriend. Little did she know how he spent his days! He looked at Maxine and relaxed; she was happy. Her face was calm as she smiled at him. Obviously she had not thought he was too sensitive or too girly when he had told her about Jay. In fact, she was acting as though he had never said a word about her. Her red hair glinted in the sunlight, and he realised that she was pretty too, in a similar way to Jay. She was attractive. He realised he was drawn to her, as he had been to Jay. He hugged her, half giving in to his impulses and half for show; his mother was still watching. On second thought, he pulled her in closer and kissed her gently. He then glanced over and made eye contact with his mum before escaping down the road, running from Max's indignation.

Alex slowed down as he neared the end of the street. He never ran as slowly as this. He was still deep in thought when they reached the motorway. He wanted to tell Max everything, from start to finish. He wanted to let her into his life, his whole life. He suddenly felt an urge to tell her about his dad and their relationship – the fact that his dad had just walked out on them a few days ago. He reined in his thoughts as he looked at Max. The look in her eyes shattered his serious thoughts; it was clear she wanted fun today, not to hear more of his emotional baggage. He decided to forget about it and take advantage of the beautiful day and the gorgeous Maxine that he had all to himself.

Death's plan was ready, but he waited for a few minutes before he summoned one of his acquaintances. Once he had

checked exactly what was happening down on earth, he called
for Cupid. The little angel was very glad to be summoned by so
great a master and such an important person, and he did not
hesitate to tell Death so. After a few minutes of his futile, fawning
babble, Death silenced him and told him what he was to do.
Cupid smiled, a sickly sweet smile, and nodded slowly. He adored
his job, especially when it was to help someone else. As he bowed
out of Death's presence subserviently, Cupid's thoughts were less
than flattering. After all, had Death not noticed that Cupid had
been very hard at work for the past few days – in exactly the place
where Death had asked him to focus?

Maxine flung her bag down, but Alex picked it up and said
that they would not come back this way so that she should
take it. She smiled up at him and put it back on her back,
strapped it on tight, and off they went, racing down the hard
shoulder, right past the A road they usually taunted cars on.
It was only when they walked down the grassy verge that
she remembered that the only thing worth doing or seeing
past the end of the motorway was his special place. They
slowed down gradually as they approached the island, and
Alex reached for her hand. They were both smiling, out of
breath and very happy. He led her to the drainpipe and asked
her if she wanted to go across. She just grinned up at him
and nodded. She wanted to see the island again – maybe she
could live there!

Alex couldn't explain the surge of emotions he felt. This
was different from when he was with Jay. She had been his
best friend, and there had never been any other thoughts
involved – not until their last day together – and even then,
they had both brushed them off and ignored them.

His heart leapt again as he looked at Maxine, and his lips searched for hers and pressed down on them. Her body had resisted when he had kissed her outside his house, but Alex had attributed that to his mum's obvious presence at the window. Now she resisted again and pushed his face away gently, briefly pressing her forehead to his lips instead. She lifted her arms to put them around his neck and let his arms lock around her waist.

"How?" was all she said. Alex knew what she was asking. He had finished off his story too curtly and had left her with no ending – but he had no satisfactory ending for her. How could he tell her without all the blame coming back, the guilt, the self-loathing he had gone through? Max watched as Alex's eyes clouded over, and she could see the pain flashing across his face, the regret, the hatred, the shame. She lowered her gaze and lay her head on his shoulder for an instant. Impulsively she reached up to kiss him, making herself trust that he would take care of her. Cupid had done his work well.

Alex looked at her and hoped her question needed no answer. He flashed her a smile before tugging at her hand like a child, and pulling her towards the pipe. Then, suddenly, he changed his mind, and he pulled her back towards him. She pressed her body against his, and he felt her warmth spread all over him. She had made it past his barriers; he could not believe it! She had got to where Jay had been and had supplanted her in Alex's affections. He had never touched Jay like this, and she would never have allowed him to do so. He kissed Maxine repeatedly, not wanting to release her but knowing that he had to. He finally disengaged himself but still held onto her hand.

The island was no longer the focus of his attention, so Alex led her by a different route, through the thicket to a long bridge that went over the motorway just before its end. The bridge had a small ledge that ran alongside it. It was terribly narrow but flatter than the gantry he was used to. He looked at Max with eyes full of love and passion. He had done this with Jay, the day she had died, and he had never been back. The memories had overwhelmed him every time he had tried.

This was the right day to do it, he decided. They would cross over on the ledge together, and then things would change for the better. Alex pulled her tight and they both stared at the bridge. The threat of falling onto the motorway compared to landing in the icy river was definitely a challenge, but if Jay had been able to do it with him, then so could his new friend. He decided he would tell her everything from start to finish when they arrived at the other end. They would have a clean beginning, a fresh start to their relationship. There was no going back now!

He turned his eyes back to Max and raised his eyebrows to ask if she dared cross. She stepped out bravely onto the ledge and tested it. She turned around on it and looked at him quizzically. She came back to him, and their bodies pressed together for the last time.

They felt their way forward, shuffling along slowly and carefully. Max went first, one hand behind her back, holding onto his, the other outstretched to balance. Her eyes were fixed on the ledge. The two inched their way towards the middle. Unseen by them, a dark figure gleefully approached them from the other side.

As they got right to the centre, Maxine clutched Alex's hand more tightly. She could see something shadowy slowly bearing down on them – what was it? A few seconds later, Max screamed as she slipped and hurtled down towards the motorway, pulling Alex with her. This was the final encounter between Alex and Death.